MEG'S CASTLE

for Stewart

MEG'S CASTLE

by Helen Nicoll
and Jan Pieńkowski

PUFFIN BOOKS

Meg, Mog and Owl
went to stay in a castle

They climbed up the spiral stairs

and
got into
a four poster bed

In the night

MOAN CLANK

they heard weird noises

Meg made a spell

The ghost vanished

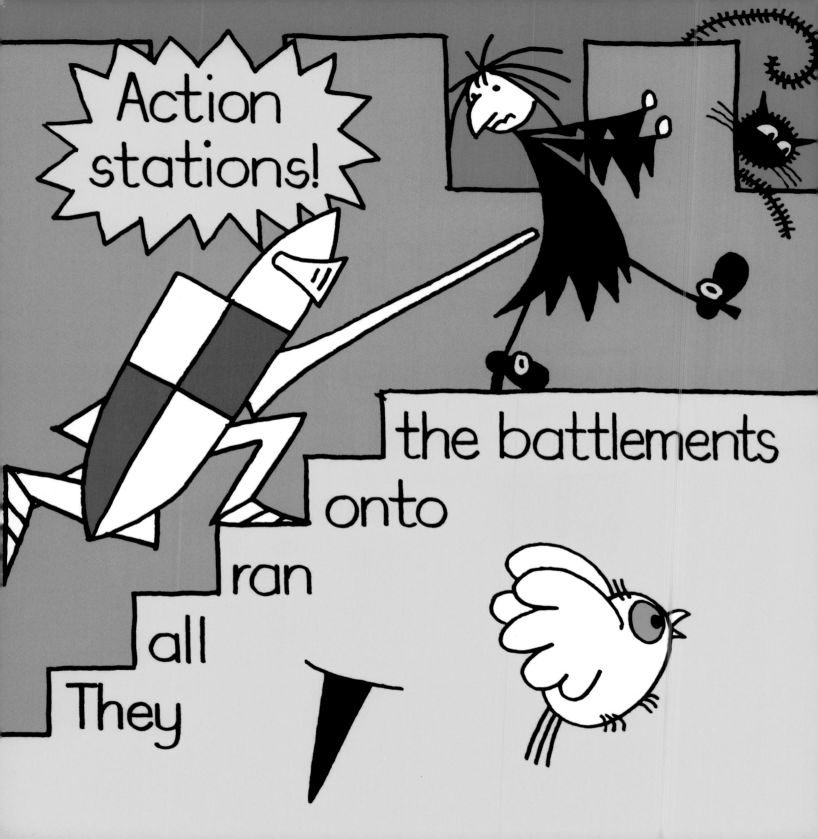

CHARGE

A green knight appeared

GALLOP GALLOP

just in time

Mog
shot
an
arrow

TWANG

and
poured
it
over
the
battlements

CRASH
OUCH

Owl
heaved
rocks
over
the
edge

The
green
knight
ran
away

They
had
a
feast
to
celebrate

After
the
feast
Meg
Mog
and
Owl
flew
home

Goodbye!